Know Thyself:

A Kid's Guide to the Archetypes

by Kiersten Marek, LICSW   Illustrations by Katrina Marek

An Identity Development Workbook

Know Thyself: A Kid's Guide to the Archetypes.
Please visit http://kierstenmarek.com for more information.

All information presented in *Know Thyself: A Kid's Guide to the Archetypes* is for informational purposes only. It is not intended as specific medical advice for any individual, and is not intended to diagnose, treat, cure, or prevent any disease. Please seek the advice of a health care professional for your specific health concerns.

ISBN 978-1-105-72090-1

Dedication

For my husband, Kevin, and my daughters, Katrina and Kalliana,
and for children everywhere who are discovering themselves.

Acknowledgements

I am grateful for the inspiration of many authors and thinkers who have influenced and guided my conception of the archetypes. They include the founder of depth psychology, Carl Jung, as well as the works of Carol S. Pearson, James Hillman, Bernice Hill, and Christine Downing. I am also particularly thankful for therapy models and theories developed by Abraham Maslow, Marsha Linehan, and Richard Schwartz.

I must also thank my friends and mentors who reviewed early drafts of this manuscript, particularly Kathryn Kulpa, Mary Callahan, Mary Beth Rua-Larsen, Tim Lehnert, Heather Thibodeau, Brian Hull, and my sister Laura Reave. Their support, encouragement, and suggestions made it possible for me to further develop my work.

This book owes its genesis to the illustrations created by my older daughter, Katrina Marek. These illustrations helped me rediscover the power of simple imagery to evoke strong emotions and important, life-changing discussions. I also want to thank my younger daughter, Kalliana, who colored the pictures for both the front and back covers beautifully.

Finally, I want to thank my clients, both children and adults, who saw and colored and responded to early drafts of this book.

What are Archetypes?

Archetypes are the ways we behave and the feelings we have. They are found in the attitudes we express toward ourselves and others. They also appear in symbols, stories, dreams, movies, books, and games. Anywhere people are living and interacting, archetypes are at play.

Have you ever had a fight with someone? You may have been experiencing the Warrior archetype -- the part of you that does battle.

Have you ever had a tender feeling when holding a baby animal? This may have been your Caregiver archetype expressing itself.

Have you ever felt sorry for someone else? The Guru archetype has the ability to see things from another person's point-of-view, and appreciate what they are going through.

Archetypes can be both healthy and unhealthy. Your healthy Warrior might fight to protect you in a situation where you are being treated unfairly. Your unhealthy Warrior might get you into constant fights with others over small issues and leave you feeling exhausted and angry.

As you go through this book, remember there are no right or wrong answers. All of the responses you give are right for you.

Why Know your Archetypes?

Knowing your archetypes makes you stronger and smarter. It helps you figure yourself out and understand other people better. It helps you organize your own experience, be a trusted friend and family member, and pursue life goals.

FUN FACT: A Swiss psychiatrist named Carl Jung first wrote about the archetypes in 1919. Dr. Jung realized that reflecting on the archetypes and talking about feelings made him and others feel better -- more aware, organized, connected, and prepared.

Ways to Use this Book

1. Color the pictures in this book. Coloring is a calming, focusing activity that stimulates your senses. You can use crayons, colored pencils, or markers.

2. After coloring the pictures, rate yourself on a scale of 1 to 10 in terms of how much you connect with the feeling of each picture. Score yourself "1" if you don't feel connected at all with the picture, and "10" if you feel very connected with the picture.

3. Write notes around the picture or in the space below -- describe how and when you feel like that picture. What do you like or dislike in the picture?

4. Come back to this book after a month and look at the pictures again. Rate how much you identify with each picture again, noticing if there is any change in how you feel about each.

5. Think about the people in your life -- friends, relatives, classmates. Do any of the images in the book remind you of certain people?

6. Share this book with a friend and have them rate the archetypes. Compare how you both rated, and discuss whether you think your ratings are accurate.

7. Use this book as a way of coping with strong feelings. When you are feeling sad, mad, or afraid, look through the book. Spend some time coloring or writing about your feelings.

The Innocent

The Innocent is the deeply curious part of every person.

Have you ever been amazed at the beauty of a flower? Have you ever heard a song that made your eyes well up with tears? Have you ever enjoyed the taste of a freshly-picked apple? We all use our senses -- sight, sound, taste, touch, and smell -- to understand life. The Innocent is all about using our senses to satisfy our curiosity for life.

When you are expressing your Innocent, you are feeling safe and protected and free to let your senses take in life. You are feeling trusting and open to new experiences.

Ways to Explore Your Innocent

1. Get some sunshine! Getting outdoors is great for your Innocent. Plus, sunshine activates Vitamin D, an important vitamin for your health.

2. Watch or play with an animal. Animals can show us how to be innocent again.

3. Practice meditation. Sit quietly somewhere and practice being aware of your senses -- sight, sound, taste, touch, and smell.

FAMOUS QUOTE: "People get dirty through too much civilization. Whenever we touch nature, we get clean." -- Carl Jung

Notes About Your Innocent:_____

_____

_____

_____

Rate Your Innocent! On a Scale of 1-10, how much do you feel like the
Innocent: 1   2   3   4   5   6   7   8   9   10

The Wounded Child

The Wounded Child is a deep sense we all have sometimes of being alone, and having no one on our side who can keep us safe or protect us from life's difficulties. The Wounded Child can be triggered by a death, conflict, ending a relationship, or an illness. It can also be triggered if someone hurts you, or if you see someone being hurt.

Why is it Good to be Aware of Your Wounded Child?

Once you are aware of your Wounded Child, you can get help. You can band together with other people who have the same feeling. You can begin to feel better so that the problem doesn't bother you as much. Best of all, you can find solutions to some problems so they won't happen again.

Ways to Explore your Wounded Child

1. Ask your parents to help you join a cause that makes the world a better and more caring place. Donate food for a food drive, or volunteer to help at a pet shelter or soup kitchen.

2. Write about the experience that brought out your Wounded Child. Then write back to yourself, expressing sympathy for all you have gone through.

3. Think of a time when someone "pushed your button" and made you feel alone. Now imagine that time again, except now, cut the wires on the button. Respond with a joke or a new topic.

FAMOUS QUOTE: "Loneliness and the feeling of being unwanted is the most terrible poverty." --Mother Theresa

Notes About Your Wounded Child:_____

_____

_____

_____

Rate Your Wounded Child! On a scale of 1-10, how much do you feel like the Wounded Child: 1   2   3   4   5   6   7   8   9   10

The Warrior

The Warrior is acting in us when we feel a deep need to make things right. This "need to be right" can lead to conflict. To have good relationships, we must be able to work out conflicts. Sometimes that means reflecting on what you did to cause the problem. Sometimes it means talking with the other person to find out what they are going through. Sometimes it means getting help from someone else to resolve things, or ending the relationship.

Sometimes our Warrior helps us take on battles inside ourselves. Maybe you want to be on the basketball team, and push yourself to practice every day before the try-outs. Your Warrior can help keep you on track to reach your goal.

Ways to Explore Your Warrior

1. Talk to your Warrior. What does it want? What is it upset about?

2. Remember that you can always retreat or step back. Retreating is an important way to work on your strategy, and it may help you find a better way to approach the situation.

3. Find ways to express your Warrior through activities that teach strategy and build strength and stamina. Sports, dance, martial arts, or any focused activity can help you build your Warrior.

FAMOUS QUOTE: "The essence of warriorship, or the essence of human bravery, is refusing to give up on anyone or anything." Chogyam Trungpa

Notes About Your Warrior: _____

_____

_____

_____

Rate your Warrior! On a scale of 1-10, how much do you feel like the Warrior: 1   2   3   4   5   6   7   8   9   10

The Caregiver

The Caregiver is the part of us that wants to nurture others. Caregiving is some of the most important work that is done in the world. It involves many roles like being a parent who protects a child, as well as being a nurse who cares for someone's health. Caregiving creates stability through comfort. Caregiving can be a form of healing.

Caring for yourself is also an important role for the Caregiver. When you brush your teeth, eat good foods, and make sure you are getting enough rest, you are being your own Caregiver.

When is Caregiving not good? Sometimes caregiving can be "too much" and can result in problems. Sometimes if you are caring too much for other people, you never figure out what YOU want. Sometimes you can wear yourself out trying to take care of other people.

Ways to Explore your Caregiver

1. Who are the caregivers in your life? Your parents? Aunts and uncles? Teachers? Friends? Think about how the Caregiver is expressed in the people in your life.

2. Write a thank you card for one of the Caregivers in your life.

3. Is there anyone in your life who needs more care? Reach out to that person.

FAMOUS QUOTE: "Blessed is the influence of one true, loving human soul on another." -- Mary Anne Evans

Notes About Your Caregiver:_____
_____
_____
_____

Rate your Caregiver! On a scale of 1-10, how much do you feel like the Caregiver: 1   2   3   4   5   6   7   8   9   10

The Explorer

The Explorer is the dreamer in all of us. It is the part that loves adventure. Explorers love to travel, meet new people, and contemplate new ideas. The Explorer likes to do experiments in order to see what happens. Each time our Explorer tries something new, our internal database grows, like a laptop adding new files and downloads. The Explorer also likes to imagine the past through history, and imagine the future through fantasy.

The Explorer can help you deal with disappointment or distress by giving you a place to escape to. Sometimes TV, movies, and books give us a chance to express our Explorer as we identify with the story's hero going on a journey and overcoming obstacles.

Ways to Access Your Explorer

1. Learn about the history of your family by asking parents and other relatives about where your family came from, and memories from their lives. Our Explorer can learn and grow by hearing about history and life experiences of others.

2. Join a club to share your particular interest with others and learn more together.

3. Is there a journey you would like to take? A place you would like to go? Why? Plan a journey close to home to let your Explorer express itself.

FAMOUS QUOTE: "Always remember it's simply not an adventure worth telling if there aren't any dragons." -- Sarah Ban Breathnach

Notes About Your Explorer:_____

_____

_____

_____

Rate your Explorer! On a scale of 1-10, how much do you feel like the Explorer: 1   2   3   4   5   6   7   8   9   10

The Soul Mate

The Soul Mate is the part of us that has a deep need for bonding. When we are born, we bond with our family. As we grow, we begin to express our Soul Mate in friendships. When we are old enough, the Soul Mate is the part of us that feels deeply connected to another person and wants to be with that person for a lifetime.

Loving ourselves is also an important role for the Soul Mate. Reading this book is helping you to be your own Soul Mate, by helping you get to know yourself more fully.

The Danger Zone for Soul Mates

Sometimes when our Soul Mate is active, it feels hard to set limits. We can feel swallowed up in a new relationship and unable to resist the influence of it. You may have extreme feelings of jealousy, or you may feel obsessed with the relationship. Get help from a trusted adult by letting them know what you are going through.

Ways to Explore your Soul Mate:

1. What do you look for the most in your friends? Is it kindness? Loyalty? The way they make you laugh? Write a list of all the things you like most about your friends.

2. Write a letter to a friend telling him or her what makes your relationship special. You might not want to give him or her the letter, but it is a good way to find out what you value in the relationship.

3. Spend time with a close friend!

FAMOUS QUOTE: "Love makes your soul crawl out from its hiding place." -- Zora Neale Hurston

Notes About Your Soul Mate:_____

_____

_____

_____

Rate your Soul Mate! On a scale of 1-10, how much do you feel like the Soul Mate:1   2   3   4   5   6   7   8   9   10

The Destroyer

The Destroyer is the strong urge in all of us for change. Sometimes we need to destroy the old to make room for the new. That's the healthy destroyer -- the one that pushes us forward in life.

But there is also an unhealthy destroyer. It is the part of us that lashes out when we are disappointed, or that wants to get back at someone for hurting us, and so we hurt them back. Or we do something to hurt ourselves. Have you ever had the urge to do something hurtful?

Ways to Use Your Healthy Destroyer:

1. Clean out your room or desk! Throw out all the things you don't need anymore, or give them away.

2. Choose your friends carefully, and end friendships that are not healthy for you.

3. Make a resolution to stop a bad habit such as biting your nails. Destroy the old way with a healthier way to soothe yourself.

Ways to Calm Your Unhealthy Destroyer:

1. Remind yourself that it is normal to feel destructive sometimes. Most moods can be changed by doing something else.

2. Try reading, exercising, or singing a favorite song in your head.

3. Write down your angry destroyer feelings. Then tear up the piece of paper and throw it away. Now draw a picture or write about something that calms you.

FAMOUS QUOTE: "To change, and to change for the better are two different things." -- German Proverb

Notes About Your Destroyer:_____

_____

_____

_____

Rate your Destroyer! On a scale of 1-10, how much do you feel like the Destroyer: 1   2   3   4   5   6   7   8   9   10

The Artist

The Artist is the part of the us that makes life new with our own creations. Maybe you make up songs and sing them for yourself or friends. Maybe you paint or draw. Maybe you create new foods by trying out things in the kitchen. These are all ways the Artist is being expressed through you.

Artists use imagination, skill, and control. They start with an idea of what they want to create and then invest their energy in creating it. Expressing your Artist can help resolve difficult feelings and give you a healthy outlet for distress.

Ways to Explore Your Artist

1. Writing in a journal -- poems, stories, songs, or just reflections on daily life are ways we make sense of reality. By naming our experiences and feelings, we understand ourselves and the world better.

2. Drawing, Painting or Sculpting -- Use Play-Doh, clay, paints, markers, colored pencils, or crayons to create.

3. Building with blocks, cooking and baking, starting a business, starting a new club, designing a website -- there are many ways to create.

4. Dressing up -- Using your imagination to dress with your own style is another way to express your artist.

FAMOUS QUOTE: "Art enables us to find ourselves and lose ourselves at the same time." -- Thomas Merton

Notes About Your Artist:_____

_____

_____

_____

Rate your Artist! On a scale of 1-10, how much do you feel like the Artist: 1   2   3   4   5   6   7   8   9   10

The Guru

The Guru is the part of us that wants to understand the world. It is the "wise" part of our being that seeks truth. Guru moments are often "A-ha!" moments when we realize something new about ourselves, someone else, or the world.

When we become aware of how everyone sees the world from a different point-of-view, we are experiencing the Guru. The Guru is able to tolerate difference and learns to let go of struggle. By doing so, the Guru becomes open to new knowledge and growth.

Beware of the False Guru

Have you ever met someone who you thought was knowledgeable and wise, and then learned that they were not all you thought they were? Sometimes people who seem to "know it all" are deceiving others with false promises.

Ways to Explore your Guru

1. Think of a time when you disagreed with someone. Why did you disagree? Now imagine you are that person. Imagine as much as you can about their daily life, things that stress them out, things that they feel good about. Think about how you accept this person, even if you disagree.

2. Look up famous quotes from someone you consider "wise." Write them in a journal and reflect on them.

3. Provide a wise quote to a friend who is going through a difficult experience.

FAMOUS QUOTE: "When you start to develop your powers of empathy and imagination, the whole world opens up to you." -- Susan Sarandon

Notes About Your Guru:_____

_____

_____

_____

Rate your Guru! On a scale of 1-10, how much do you feel like the Guru: 1   2   3   4   5   6   7   8   9   10

The Leader

The Leader is the part of us that knows how to oversee our lives and make adjustments to bring about more harmony and prosperity. The Leader is like a mini president of a company inside your head who works to make things the way you want them to be. The Leader knows we have to make choices, and helps us look at the whole picture before making those choices.

If our Leader is too strong, we may be rigid and controlling, and in danger of hurting ourselves or others. Remember that dominating is not the same thing as leading.

If our Leader is too weak, we may not feel we have enough control over our lives. We may feel like we are being pushed around by other forces or people. If this is the case, your Leader needs to express itself more.

Ways to Explore your Leader

1. Design a town. Start by thinking of a name for your town, and then try mapping things out on paper -- houses, parks, stores. Make sure you include places for fun, work, and learning. Keep adding on until you have all the things you want and need in your town.

2. Think of what the rules are that are most important in your life. Make a list of them.

3. Design an ideal daily schedule for yourself-- doing exactly what you want. Make sure you include all of the necessary parts, like exercising, free time, bath or shower time, and times for meals.

FAMOUS QUOTE: "Leadership is a series of behaviors rather than a role for heroes." -- Margaret Wheatley

Notes About Your Leader: _____

_____

_____

_____

Rate your Leader! On a scale of 1-10, how much do you feel like the Leader: 1   2   3   4   5   6   7   8   9   10

The Healer

The Healer is the part of us that can change ourselves or the world. It is the part that can restore health to ourselves when we have been hurt, and can help others heal. The Healer is aware that we are all connected to each other, and connected to the whole.

Being a Healer means that you pay close attention to a problem and use your thoughtfulness, experience, and insight to bring about positive change. Maybe a friend comes to you with a problem, and by listening carefully, you are able to help your friend realize what they need to do to solve the problem. You have just been a healing force in your friend's life!

Ways to Access your Healer

1. Meditating -- by focusing inward and being aware of your thoughts and your breathing, you can become more connected to your internal power.

2. Ritual Mantras -- use a short phrase to remind yourself of your gifts and powers. Example: "I have everything I need and I care about myself and others."

3. Change a Negative into a Positive -- if you find yourself thinking something negative such as, "I can't play soccer!" change it up so that it is in present tense and supportive of your goals: "I am practicing and getting better all the time."

FAMOUS QUOTE: "Whatever you think you can do or believe you can do, begin it. Action has magic, grace and power in it." -- Johann Wolfgang

Notes About Your Healer: _____

_____

_____

_____

Rate your Healer! On a Scale of 1-10, how much you feel like the Healer: 1   2   3   4   5   6   7   8   9   10

The Fool

The Fool and the Innocent are alike in many ways. The Fool is the part that returns us to the beginning -- finding joy and laughter in all of life's sensory experiences. The Fool is also the rule-breaker -- the part of us that clowns around and pokes fun at the Warrior and Ruler when they are being too serious.

The Fool loves freedom above all else, and wants to follow bliss wherever it might lead. Fools like to experiment and explore, and to use their imaginations. The Fool is sometimes the part that thinks up something fun to do when you are bored.

Beware the Negative Fool

If we are not aware of our Fool, it can come out in unhealthy ways, breaking important rules and doing things that are wrong and hurtful. Remember: your Fool, like your Destroyer, must be fed to be kept calm. That's why you need to let yourself have fun and enjoy good times. If you try to starve your fool, it can become difficult to manage.

FAMOUS QUOTE: "A fool thinks himself to be wise, but a wise man knows himself to be a fool." -- William Shakespeare

Notes About Your Fool:_____

_____

_____

_____

Rate your Fool! On a Scale of 1-10, how much you feel like the Fool:
1   2   3   4   5   6   7   8   9   10

A Note About the Sequence of the Archetypes

There are 12 archetypes in this book. Each one has similarities to the others, yet each one is unique.

The archetypes can appear in any order, but a typical life might follow the sequence presented in this book.

The First Four -- the Innocent, the Wounded Child, the Warrior, and the Caregiver -- are usually more present in Childhood.

The Middle Four -- the Explorer, the Soul Mate, the Destroyer, the Artist -- are usually more present in Adolescence.

The Final Four -- the Guru, the Leader, the Healer, and the Fool -- are usually more present in Adulthood.

As you go through this book, think about yourself as well as the people in your family and community, and times when you have experienced the archetypes. Whatever stage of life you are at, it is important to know about all 12 of the archetypes so you can be prepared for life's journey.

Note to Parents

Thank you for helping your child learn more about all of the aspects of themselves. Offering your child acceptance of their archetypes is one of the best gifts you can give them as a parent. Angry destroyer moments in children are just as much a part of them as moments of serene innocence, and your ability to offer acceptance to all aspects of their identity is key to fostering their emotional growth and stability, as well as a strong and enduring parent-child bond.

I believe as parents we have important stories to tell our children from our own life experiences, and the archetypes in this book may help you to retrieve and express some of these experiences. Sharing with your child about your own experiences will help your child feel more connected to you.

As you look through this book, take the opportunity to reflect on your own experiences of the archetypes. For example, a memory you might share about your Innocent could describe how you played as a child and what kinds of outdoor activities you enjoyed. For the Warrior, you might reflect on a time as a child when you got into conflict.

Some of the experiences that come up for you as you explore your archetypes may not be appropriate for your child to know about. They may be too scary, may involve adult content, or may bring up emotional issues that are too complex for your child to understand.

I encourage parents to share, but to choose carefully which stories they share. Be aware of how your child is responding to what you are sharing, and keep your story at a level that they can understand and that will not overwhelm them.

Note to Therapists

This workbook can function both as a data collection tool in sessions, and as homework for children to do either alone or with a parent. With smaller children, you can help them fill in the "notes" section by writing for them and helping them to understand the scale. They can color the book in session while you talk about the archetypes, or use the archetypes to lead into dialogue about family issues, school issues, or feelings exploration and education. Taking out the workbook and making additional notes or comments in future sessions is a good way to note changes in behavior or emotional expression and reinforce important messages related to the treatment plan.

It is important to realize that the archetypes that come later in the series are generally not as present in small children (ages 3 to 10). The Leader, the Healer, and the Guru are generally expressions of a more whole and complex identity than most small children express. However, the roots of their expression can be fostered, as well as an appreciation for their importance.

On Interpreting the Rating Scale: The 1-10 rating scale for the archetypes can help you gauge how extreme a child's feelings are about each archetype. When a child gives a very high or low rating to an archetype, it may mean this part of their identity needs more attention. Each picture and its accompanying text can be used as a discussion tool. Your response or comment on the picture can help a dialogue develop that will bring out more detailed information about a child's mental and emotional states.

It is not uncommon for children who have suffered abuse and neglect to rate the Wounded Child as a "1" or deny having any feelings associated with their Wounded Child. Similarly, some children with aggressive behavior problems will deny feeling any connection with the Destroyer. This gives you important information about how difficult it is for them to see and accept their experiences.

Returning to the pictures with the child when they experience a new episode that triggers their Destroyer or their Wounded Child may help them build self-awareness and work toward changing problem behaviors. When you return to these images, be sure to also review some of the archetypes in the book that they have a positive connection with, and talk about how these parts can help them to change their behavior, cope with feelings, or communicate with others to solve the problem.

CPSIA information can be obtained
at www.ICGtesting.com
Printed in the USA
LVHW01s0114201217
560334LV00028B/2310/P